FROSTY
KINGDOM

This frosty fairy-tale adventure belongs to

....

LADYBIRD BOOKS

UK | USA | Canada | Ireland | Australia | India | New Zealand | South Africa

Ladybird Books is part of the Penguin Random House group of companies
whose addresses can be found at global.penguinrandomhouse.com.

www.penguin.co.uk   www.puffin.co.uk   www.ladybird.co.uk

Penguin
Random House
UK

First published 2019
001

Printed in China

A CIP catalogue record for this book is available from the British Library

ISBN: 978-0-241-41766-9

All correspondence to:
Ladybird Books
Penguin Random House Children's
80 Strand, London WC2R 0RL

MIX
Paper from
responsible sources
FSC
www.fsc.org
FSC® C018179

Peppa's Frosty Fairy Tale

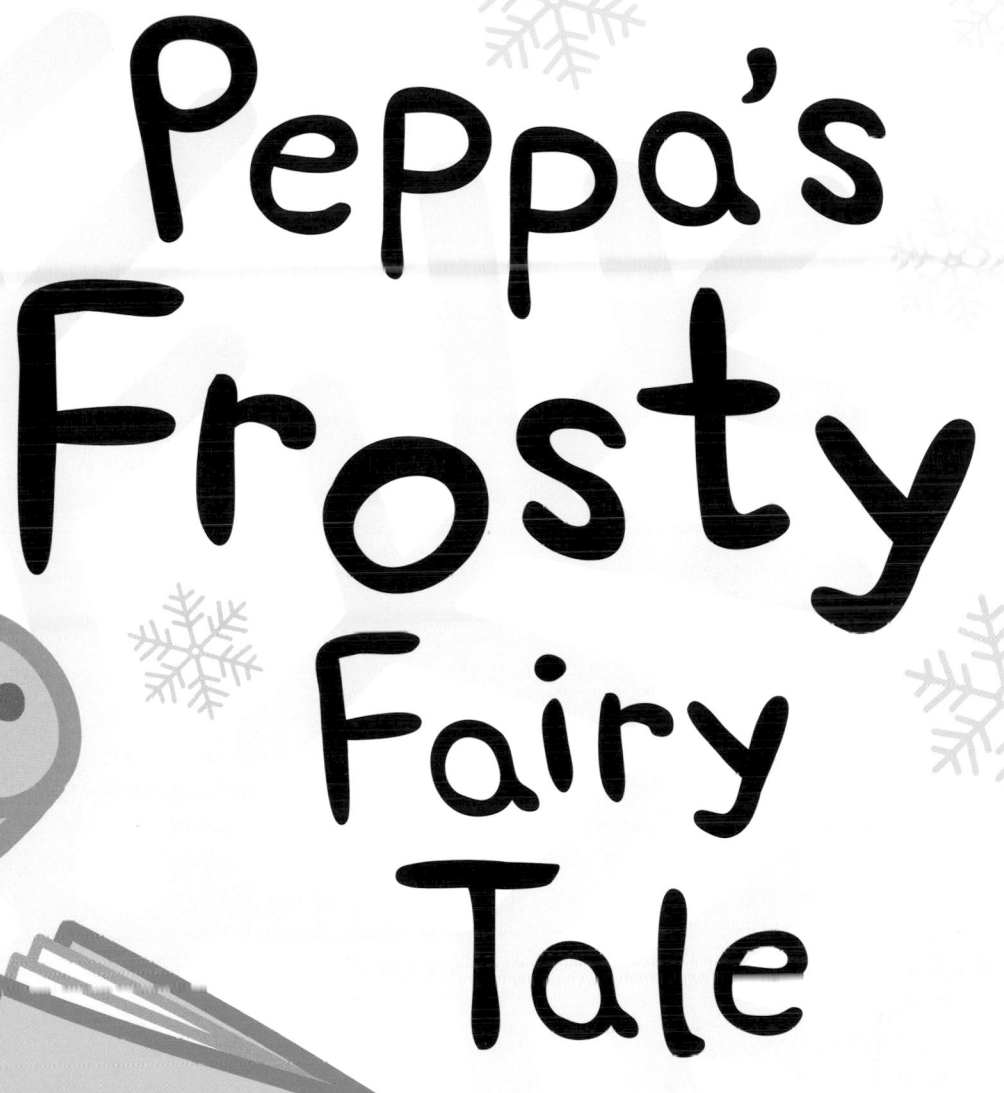

Once upon a time, it was a cold and quiet winter's day. Peppa and George were playing indoors and making lots of noise.

"Peppa! George!" called Mummy Pig.
"Why don't you look in your box of books
and pick a nice story to read?"

Peppa and George searched through the box and pulled out their favourite books. They giggled with excitement as they looked through the pages.

Then, Peppa danced all over the living room,
pretending she was in a fairy tale.
"A sno-man!" cheered George, holding his favourite book.
Peppa and George loved stories.

That evening, Granny and Grandpa Pig came over to stay the night.
"Hello, Granny and Grandpa!" said Peppa and George.
"Hello, little ones," said Granny Pig, giving them both a big hug.

"It's time for bed now," said Mummy Pig.
"Please can Granny and Grandpa tell us a bedtime story?" asked Peppa.
"Of course, Peppa," said Granny Pig. "We'd love to."

Once Peppa and George were tucked up in bed, Grandpa Pig showed them a beautiful snow globe. Then, he began to tell a story.

"Once upon a time," he said, "there was a cold and magical place called Frosty Kingdom . . ."

"How do you get to Frosty Kingdom?" asked Peppa.
"First, you have to travel over the snowy hills," said Grandpa Pig.
"Then, you journey through a deep, dark forest. Finally, you
must climb a huge mountain, until you reach
the winter castle at the very top."

"I bet the Sugar Plum Fairy lives there, and a snow queen!" said Peppa.
"Sno-man!" said George.
Peppa and George loved Grandpa Pig's story.
"I wish we could go to Frosty Kingdom, too," said Peppa, as she
and George drifted off to sleep.

Jingle! Jingle! Jingle!

In the morning, Peppa and George woke up to the sound of jingling bells. They peered through the window to find out where the noise was coming from. "It's snowing!" gasped Peppa. "And Granny and Grandpa are outside with a big sleigh . . . and three reindeers!"

Just then, Mummy and Daddy Pig came into the bedroom.
"Granny and Grandpa are taking us all on an adventure,"
said Mummy Pig. "We're going to Frosty Kingdom!"
"Frosty Kingdom was in Grandpa's story!" said Peppa.

"We'll be needing these," said Mummy Pig, handing out
winter coats and woolly jumpers. "We're travelling by sleigh."
"Hooray!" cheered Peppa and George, jumping up and down.

Everyone climbed into the sleigh, and they set off.
"Which way is Frosty Kingdom?" asked Daddy Pig.
Grandpa Pig pointed far into the distance. "First, you have
to travel over the snowy hills . . ." he began.

"...Then, you journey through a deep, dark forest," said Peppa. "Finally, you must climb a huge mountain, until you reach the winter castle at the very top."

"That's right, Peppa!" said Grandpa Pig.

FROSTY KINGDOM

After they went over the snowy hills and
through the deep, dark forest, they started
to climb the huge mountain.
"Are we nearly there yet?" asked Peppa.
Suddenly, George saw something move.
"Sno-man!" he squealed.

Everyone turned to see
a snowman waving at them.
"Hello," said Peppa. "We are on our
way to Frosty Kingdom!"
Peppa and George waved goodbye
and the reindeers pulled the sleigh
further up the mountain.

FROSTY
KINGDOM

Up the mountain they climbed. Up and up and up, until the sleigh reached a clearing and the reindeers stopped.
"Are we nearly there now?" asked Peppa.
"I can't see the magical winter castle!"

"I think we may be lost . . ." said Grandpa Pig.
"I'm sure it was this way!"
"Oh no!" Peppa sighed. "What are we going to do?"
"If only there was someone here to help,"
said Grandpa Pig.

"Hello, Peppa and George!" a voice said.
"Look, it's Miss Rabbit!" said Peppa.
"Actually, Peppa, I'm the Sugar Plum Fairy," said Miss Rabbit.
"You're on the right path. Frosty Kingdom is further
up the mountain!"
"This is so magical!" cried Peppa.

FROSTY
KINGDOM

The sleigh climbed higher once more, and was nearly at the top of the mountain, when . . .

"Welcome to Mr Fox's Official Frosty Kingdom Shop!" said Mr Fox. Everyone hopped off the sleigh to take a quick look around.

Daddy Pig loaded up a basket with sponges, telephones and wool. "I'm sure these will come in handy at Frosty Kingdom!" he said. Everyone piled back on the sleigh and they set off yet again.

Finally, they arrived at Frosty Kingdom.
"We're here!" announced Grandpa Pig.
Peppa saw something sparkling up ahead.
As they got nearer, she gasped. "It's the winter castle
and there's the Snow Queen! Look, it's Miss . . ."

Hee!
Hee!

"Hello, everyone," interrupted Miss Rabbit.
"I'm the Snow Queen. Welcome to Frosty Kingdom!"
Peppa and George waved and giggled excitedly.

WELCOME TO
FROSTY
KINGDOM

"I wish we could stay here," said Peppa.

"Peppa, this is our cabin!" said Grandpa Pig.

"We're going to stay here for the night."

"Wow!" cried Peppa. "This is the best frosty fairy-tale adventure ever! Thank you, Granny and Grandpa!"

"Ho! Ho! You're most welcome," said Grandpa Pig, smiling.

Peppa and George raced inside the
cabin and looked around excitedly.
"It's like we're in your story!" cried Peppa.
"Maybe we are!" said Grandpa Pig, laughing.

Peppa loved frosty fairy tales.
Everyone loved frosty fairy tales!